An Impractical Guide

to

Marriage

An Impractical Guide

to

Marriage

Gabriela Anaya Valdepeña

Darkness Visible Books
La Jolla 2012

First edition published in 2012 by

Darkness Visible Books
P.O. Box 577
La Jolla, CA 92038
darknessvisiblebooks@yahoo.com

Cover photo by Gabriela Anaya Valdepeña

FIRST EDITION

Printed in the United States of America

Library of Congress Control Number: 2012930309

ISBN: 978-0-9774000-6-5

For Caslyn and Doug

Contents

Prologue

There once was a girl who longed to stay free,
quite unlike her poor mother, abandoned by three
worthless husbands, and left with six mouths to supply,
with sad prayers for romance, but no hope of reply,
who, much like the woman who lived in a shoe,
with so many children, didn't know what to do,
and frustrated in love, with her hopes fading fast
let her fairy tale dreams slip away to the past.
But must love always lead to the baby carriage?
Now it's not that our heroine, Lil, hated marriage,
but Lil, unlike Mom, proved surprisingly able
to mold out of marriage a far different fable!
No, Lily wouldn't settled for tripping on toys,
for breaking up fights, or enduring loud noise!
What Lil liked producing were husbands, not children,
especially ones who wouldn't act like it killed 'em
to cook a fine roast, just for her, if she asked,
and yet sometimes say no, even take her to task,
(since, though a curmudgeon might bring you some stress,
nothing's worse than a dullard who always says yes!)
But this very fine balance was painful to master,
so some Lil endured, and yet some she left faster

than the hand of a spinster, with fading red hair,
snatches a wedding bouquet from the air.
And so, though Lil married just one at a time,
by the time she was forty she'd had at least nine,
not counting three times she couldn't quite say "I do,"
one annulment, and broken engagement or two.
I know this may seem a hard story to swallow,
but all will be told in the nine tales that follow;
and for those prudent readers, in marriage untried,
they may prove a complete, if impractical guide.

———•◆•———

The Welder from Waco

L ike five, and like seven, Lil's first was a Virgo,
   the anal retentive, yet pot-smoking, Sam.
Shrewd readers may guess, 'stead of *cogito ergo*,
Lil's truth was *I marry, therefore I am.*

But Lily's first motives weren't quite so oblique.
She spent much of her life trying not to recall
the real reason she left dear old Harrison Creek
in the first place, the reason she married, at all!

'Twas her brother, in fact, who had made her leave town.
Lil caught him one night with his hand in the till,
caressing the cash mom was 'bout to send down
to her sister in Austin, languishing ill.

"Drop it now!" shouted Lil, "or I'll go straight to Mom,
or I'll call the police, or I'll tell uncle Sunny!"
"But Lily, don't squeal on me!" begged brother Tom,
"I'm caught in this jam 'cause I owe the mob money!"

"A mob," scoffed Lil, "in old Harrison Creek?
You and your petty delusions of grandeur!"
But Tom fled with the dough, leaving Lily to speak
to her mom, trying hard to blend sweetness with candor.

"Oh Momma," Lil cried, "I'm afraid you've been wronged,
and what's worse, by your own beloved son Thomas.
I discovered him snaking the cash that belonged
to Aunt Jan. He well knew it was already promised."

But Mom wouldn't accept that her son was a thief.
Growing mad as a vagabond vexed by a midge,
she banished poor Lily, whose shock, and whose grief,
now drove her on, blindly, to suicide bridge.

A Dickensian cloud had descended on Lil.
Without father, and now without mother, it seemed,
and shorn of her siblings, Lil brooded until
she felt more alone than she ever had dreamed.

With no friends, with no money, with dearest Aunt Dot
locked up for four weeks (for the usual prostitution),
and with hapless Aunt Jan on a hospital cot,
poor Lil could determine no other solution

than to hurtle, headfirst, to a merciful death.
So, removing hair ribbon, and last tennis shoe,
Lil straddled the rail, took one final breath,
and gazed at the water, breathtakingly blue.

Fresh out of Waco's Advanced School for Welders,
meanwhile, Sam Bennett was headed for work
in New Orleans, and dreaming of all he would build thar,
when the sight of poor Lil gave his heartstrings a jerk.

"Stay right where you are little lady!" he called.
"You can't help me," sobbed Lily. "Just leave me alone!"
"All troubles," cried Sam, "can in time be resolved.
If you jump, I'll jump too, and we'll both freeze our bones!"

"But you see," Lily wept, "I've got nowhere to go!"
"Come on down," Sam responded. "This height makes me queasy.
I've got a job prospect that pays decent dough.
You best tag along with me to the Big Easy."

Well a jump in the lake, or a ride with a stranger,
to a suicide, sounds pretty much the same game,
so Lil hopped in the car, and while stopping in Granger
for hunting and fishing, Sam made her his dame.

They were happy to sample the scents of New Orl'ns,
and settled right comfy in old Pirogue Cove.
And how Lily blessed the fortuitous ord'nance
pronouncing them regular Juno and Jove!

Sam found a job welding, for Mart' Marietta,
most happily monitoring kilopascal,
and Lil also proved to be quite the go-getta',
answering phones for a firm on Canal.

Lil learned to make gumbo, and sweet pumpkin bread,
and Sam's fav'rite delicacy, chicken fried steak.
They hung out with new friends, mainly Mimi and Fred,
and took long walks alone around Ponchatrain Lake.

When Mardi Gras came, Lily dressed as a flapper,
and Sam, as a sexy and stylish young gangster,
and when a young lout yelled he wanted to tap her,
brave Sam made short work of the drunk little wankster.

Lil cried, "No one's ever defended my honor!"
and she gave a long kiss to her valiant Sam.
"And that day on the bridge? I'd now be a goner,
if you hadn't saved me from one awful jam.

"I'm so happy with you, though I miss dear old Mom!"
Now Lil started crying, so Samuel replied,
"She chose to take sides with your dumb brother Tom.
It was not *you* who stole! It was not *you* who lied!

"Besides, it's Fat Tuesday; you're not s'posed to cry;
you're supposed to kick back." Then he pulled out some pot.
"God damn it," said Lily, "you promised you'd try
to quit that damn shit, at least that's what I thought!"

"Come on Lily!" Sam cried, "I'm not smoking that much
any more. I'm just marking a special occasion!
After all, I don't need any crippling crutch;
I've got you to relieve all my daily frustration!"

"But a toke for you, Sam, quickly turns to a habit,"
Lil reminded, "I've seen you veg out for ten days.
For you pot's like carrots to ravenous rabbits,
and I won't have you backsliding to your old ways!"

"Don't fret," Sam assured her, "you'd better believe
I ain't gonna do nothing to mess up our thing.
I'd be crazy to give you good reason to leave.
Why bogart a leaf, with a Lily to cling?"

It's true that besides the weird way he'd arrange
their record collection in odd categories,
for a number of months Sam had done nothing strange.
Still, why divide singers 'tween Lib'rals and Tories?

And why did he class her *Dan Hill* under *C*,
for *Canadian Douchebags*, beside *Bryan Adams*?
And why must her *Rush* be arranged under *G*,
For the *Greatest Canadian Bands* one could fathom?

But these were just quirks that our Lil could live with,
just so long as her Sam was not calling in sick
to toke the day long, or to knock off a fifth,
while ogling his neighbor and stroking his prick.

No more of such nonsense for faithful Sam Bennett!
"You had me," he teased, "at the two words 'I'll jump.'"
To which Lily replied, "It's so perfect now innit?"
After which the two love birds proceeded to hump.

But how soon, gentle reader, can honeymoons wane!
How soon restless thoughts can despoil the night!
Strange knocks, hidden glances, suspicions and strain
soon gather to canker young lovers' delight.

One day Lil came home to espy neighbor Susie
recumbent with Sam as they watched Dr. Who,
while sharing a joint, and soon Lil had the floosie
by dirty blonde locks, with her face in the loo.

"It's not what it looks like!" Sam pleaded with Lil.
"She just wanted to bake, and watch cheap BBC.
She knocked on our door, said she wanted to chill.
It's not like she begged, 'Won't you make love to me?'

"You're the only one for me, and that is the truth!
Susie's hooters are saggy; she has a flat ass,
and now, thanks to you, she's missing a tooth!
But oh how I treasure your moxie and sass!"

Well you know you still love'm when a few little kisses
can quiet a stubborn, perfidious storm,
erasing the shame of his stupid excuses,
and making you ripe for his promised reform.

But the heart only makes itself new for new wounds.
Very soon a new tolling was heard at the door.
This time it was Joe-Bob and Eli Calhoun,
demanding weed money, no later than four.

But Sam had been drinking, all day, down at Hank's.
He'd been fired for taking a snoozer while checking
the welds in the depths of a space shuttle tank.
(He thought he could toke there, with no one suspecting.)

By the end of the night he had spent his last check
on ten drinks, two male ferrets, and one cheap tattoo.
Lil pretended to sleep as he gave her a peck
on the cheek, then sheepishly fed on cold stew.

"I know we can't live on your wages alone,"
Sam explained the next morning, "but I'll find work soon.
And I'm glad I got fired! I felt like some drone.
 It was hopeless to keep my eyes open past noon."

But without a good reference from his old boss,
and folks calling him *Siesta Sam* all through town,
Sam's quest came to seem rather like a lost cause,
despite his own promise that soon he'd rebound.

At last he found work down at *Avery Label*,
though toiling only for minimum wage,
and he slowly went nuts, at his own kitchen table,
compiling weird lists, on page after page.

Sam labeled, and listed, and mated, and married
odd shoes and shoe boxes, old pictures and frames,
and, reading along in a slang dictionary,
began to call Lily all sorts of strange names.

"You don't mean all those things," Lily whispered to Sam.
"It's your job that is making you crazy, that's all."
"Is that so, silly slattern? I don't give a damn
for your thoughts," grunted Sam, "or for your caterwaul."

Lily struggled for months to break through to her spouse,
but could see, in the end, there was simply no use.
With the rain in her heart, and the loon in her house,
poor Lil could no longer withstand the abuse.

So she packed up her hats, said goodbye to the ferrets,
taking with her her books, and her clothes, and her grace,
leaving Sam with his faults, his occasional merits,
and his pitiful efforts to keep things in place.

———◆———

The Lily Curse

S weet Lily never once looked back,
   unlike the spouse of Lot,
but kept her eyes on Kansas, and
the road to dear Aunt Dot,
although her several husbands,
all regretful to a fault,
from Utah to El Paso, would
leave pedestals of salt.

Now Lil didn't mean to hurt them so,
but just by up and leaving,
prodded their proud and angry hearts
to paroxysms of grieving.
They'd blame on Lil, the loneliness,
the drink, and even worse,
'til therapists across the land
dubbed this *The Lily Curse*.

But Lil was an innocent and acci-
dental *femme fatale*,
ne'er listed 'mongst the vampires
in the fervid *Fleurs du Mal*,
and she, herself, was wracked with torment,
tears, and bitter trauma,
over the sad imbroglio
with brother and with momma.

So, sick with thoughts of Harrison Creek,
Lil detoured right through Texas,
anxious to glimpse her own home town
'fore heading up to Kansas.
But Lil read maps like she read men,
and wound up in Fort Worth,
lost, and alone, and hungry, craving
meal, mates, and mirth.

"Kansas is too darn far tonight,"
reflected famished Lily,
"and *Lone Star Inn* has vacancies,
and serves free bowls of chili."
So, after checking in and chowing
down, she soon retired,
then, galvanized by the Cowtown sun,
our Lil awoke inspired!

Her nimble wit was smoldering,
her every neuron firin'
at once, as Lily pressed her gingham
dress, with the motel iron,
and heading off to *Denny's*, morning
paper in her hand,
Lil gobbled grits and gravy, as
she circled and she scanned.

"*Sans saboteur*," she reasoned, "you
can make it where you want it,
and why keep on the road when you
can blossom where you flaunt it?"
So Lil soon found employment selling
ads on city maps
to restaurants, and hair salons,
and local tourist traps.

Delighted that her job didn't leave her
stuck behind a desk,
Lil bopped her grown up body, with
her smile Lolita-esque,
from Beach Street to the Stock Yards,
and neither ma'm nor mister,
who listened to her sales pitch,
could possibly resist her.

One day, Lil paused in front of *The
Executive Retreat*,
a fancy restaurant, it seemed,
that served "fine cuts of meat,"
but wondered, when she read below,
A Club for Gentlemen,
"How can they make a buck admitting
cock without the hen?"

The place was curiously dark,
and what was still more weird,
a glowing stage stood at one end,
where, suddenly, there appeared
a woman in a business suit,
dressed so professional
'twas odd to soon discover she
preferred no clothes at all!

And as the song *Hot Blooded* blared,
Lil turned to blow the joint,
but the boss, blocking her at the door,
begged, "Please don't disappoint
our beauty-loving customers!
You should at least come out
for Naughty-Nighty Amateur Night.
My card. Give me a shout!"

Now, dancing naked may not be
much worse than being wife,
and Lily was no skittish prude,
but still, she liked her life
the way it was. Although her job
was not so lucrative,
nor was her studio, it's true,
the safest place to live.

And who could blame on Lil the foolish
thoughts fate 'gan provoking,
when first her rad ran dry, and then
her brakes began a smoking,
and next, when she came home to find
her humble rental robbed?
"My TV, cash, and stereo—
all gone!" poor Lily sobbed.

In times like this, one best consult
with Jesus, or a psychic.
But Christ was deaf, or maybe just
too busy to reply quick.
The gypsy, then, foretold, "You'll win
a contest. Take first prize!"
So Lily rushed right out to buy
a nightie in her size.

And sure as Hell and *Haliburton*,
Lily won, that night,
twelve roses, two fat Benjamins,
and a case of *Miller Light*.
"I bet I'd make more money in
one evening," Lil supposed,
"than in a week of peddlin' maps,
wearing respectable clothes!"

Soon Lil was reaping Texas tips,
while stripping on the day shift,
making grown men break down in happy
tears, though some would bray, miffed
that she would never date them, 'spite
of how they would entreat.
(Lil knew that all they wanted was
to get her off her feet!)

Lil did concede her charms, at last,
to Mark, a vain *vaquero*,
who saved her from a groping drunk,
thrilling her to the marrow.
But Mark, who never left the club
himself, asked Lil to quit,
and Lil would never suffer, gladly,
fool or hypocrite.

A brilliant lad from Liverpool
soon erased that Mark,
a literary scholar (though
a hustler, and card shark).
But he was sworn to another queen,
who soon lured him back home,
with royal grants for the gallant knight
to pen a regal tome.

Finally, after knights and cowboys,
Cupid sent a clown,
a rodeo clown, that is, named Ty,
who strutted on the town
in *Members Only* jacket and
his skin tight *Wrangler* jeans.
"Is he a masochist," wondered Lil,
"or showing off his means?"

When Tyler caught a glimpse of Lil,
his jaw fell to his boots.
He couldn't take his eyes off her,
but jealous of gawking coots,
he asked, "How much to keep you, the
whole evening, at my table?
Just name your price!" he promised her,
but Lil just wasn't able

to fix a fee for hours bought
in such adoring doses,
and who can say what wage is fair,
when love itself proposes?
What woman, longing love 'bove all,
would take a poor man's bill,
when his true heart might offer far
beyond his meager till?

"I'll dally with you," Lily said,
"'til I must mount the stage.
No charge for smiles and quiet words,
though I must ask a wage
for table dances, in which case
it's twenty bucks a song,
and I can't pull my pasties off,
nor strip beyond this thong.

"And keep in mind the rules—never
fiddle with my flouncers!
Though other dancers may not care,
I'll surely call the bouncers!"
Now Tyler thought such modesty,
in such a place, quite silly,
but soon became a VIP,
and daily courted Lily.

Lil grew to love her rodeo clown,
and missed him when he left
to taunt bold bulls, and worried he'd
be bloodied and bereft
of more than polka dotted pants,
since, after too much beer,
Tyler confessed, one night, he'd lost
a part he held most dear!

Beware, oh balls, the vengeful horns
of bovines we enrage,
when, for our pleasure, they are ridden
mad across the stage!
And though a lonely ball can fully
serve its center player,
poor Ty, already insecure,
still felt a little feyer.

And spite of Lil's assurances
a missing nut didn't matter,
mercurial Ty soon metamorphed
from darling to mad hatter.
"Who did you tickle for such tips?"
he'd grill, with tortured look,
while fostering fights with regulars,
with DJ, and with cook.

Finally, in a fit, he ripped
Lil's stripper gear to rags
and tore the heels from her rainbow shoes,
demanding, "Pack your bags,
or quit your job and marry me!"
So Lil, the frightened creature,
hoping that love would conquer all,
followed him to the preacher.

You'd think that Lil would know by now
that love's no panacea,
though, quick with her "I do", she was
still quicker with her "see ya."
But Ty would not be left like that.
He threatened and he stalked her,
at work, at home, at *Taco Bell*,
the jealous motherfocker!

He begged that Lil return, or else,
to his enclosing arms,
(though courting, on the side, capricious
dames of shallow charms!)
The truth be told, that weasel was
unfaithful all along,
thinking that Lily was corrupt
as he, but thinking wrong.

But soon Lil's troubles would be over,
thanks to cowgirl Sherry,
who roped herself the clownish cad,
forcing the fool to marry
in a lavish rodeo ceremony,
south of San Antone,
Ty said "I do," with feet so cold
they chilled him to the bone.

It's rumored, to this day, that Sherry
runs a henpecked roost.
No Lil would ever come again
to give Ty's cock a boost.
He eats, he sleeps, he works, with never
a hope of dally dilly;
but thoughts run free, at times, and when
his do, they turn to Lily.

Two Down
and Seven to Go

Two down and seven to go, though Lil believed,
always, her latest would be her last. If more,
indeed, loved love like Lil, I'd have achieved
much more as wedding planner than as poor,
despised poet, peddling tales of aggrieved
lovers at wages cheaper than a whore.
Oh to enjoy a profitable post,
as planner, pander, or as cathouse host!

Alas, one must be happy with her lot—
unless her man's named Lot, then not so much!
I know, the allusion's tired, but all I've got;
my coffee's gone, and with it, so's my touch.
Balzac could write all night, but every thought
was fueled by grounds stored handy in his hutch.
(He couldn't just walk to Starbucks for his fix.)
But this poor scribbler'd love to sleep 'til six!

Yet shows go on, and stories must ensue,
with or without the joe—no time to snooze!
And if I sink into a stubborn blue,
without caffeine, at least I don't drink booze—
that is not when I write—some jerk might sue
for libels ill-disguised, and I could lose
my house, my dog, or worse, have to retract
a pretty lie I longed to pass as fact.

Still, none would fault me if I chugged some brews,
having in common with my dear Balzac
childhoods overpowered by pious shrews.
'Course he's a genius, me, an unknown hack.
'Til I'm discovered, or 'til I pay my dues,
I'm just a bard with landlord on my back,
one more neurotic writer trying to cope,
(though blushing to exploit that tired trope!)

Now, Lil was far from dipsomaniac,
(though I swear a single kiss could make her drunk,
and may God grant a sudden cardiac
if I purvey here hyperbolic junk.
Besides, why risk a superficial hack
that jealous journalists could soon debunk?
I wouldn't want dear Oprah to feel took,
when, finally, she recommends this book!)

As I was saying, Lil couldn't down one glass
of wine, nor half a dinner. She was easy
on a man's wallet as well as eyes, a lass
who drove men silly without a hint of sleazy.
Though blessed with Mae West's wiggle, and her sass,
she still preferred an evening at parcheesi.
Some crave to incandesce like Diamond Lil;
some choose less sparkle, and a smaller bill.

Of all the men, in fact, who hung upon
Lil's hopeful favors, the ones she fancied most
were men of modest means. She'd never fawn
on robber barons—those who'd boldly boast
coin over character— nor dapper don
who'd flaunt her freely and yet shut her close.
Lil couldn't be had for vulgar currency,
for sniffy airs, or snobbish duncery.

But, then again, Lil wouldn't discriminate
against a suitor just for being rich.
Money need no more spawn a proud ingrate
than fashion Lil into a Stepford bitch.
Many a saint is born to great estate;
many a sinner greets us from the ditch.
And so it was with open mind, and eye,
Lil opened her front door, to the cable guy.

And what a cable guy! Lil first looked down,
then up, then 'cross his handsome uniform,
until her unbelieving glances found,
upon his chest, the name of *William Storm*.
"Why would a man whose father owns the town
so flagrantly insult the family norm,
and trade the prince's for the pauper's perspective?"
Lil wondered, but couldn't guess at his objective.

And Lil was always taught to never pry,
(unless it be her mama's orange jam).
"Ask no man questions and no man will lie,"
repeated Mom, and Dad, and Gramps, and Gram.
Not that a curious woman can't be sly—
if you want a man's confessions, flash some gam!
No doubt, Lil's thighs would get you blathering;
some say such stems would make the muses sing!

But our sweet Lil didn't aim to flaunt her sex.
Her flawless charm was almost automatic.
She never would deliberately vex
a passing buck with fantasies ecstatic.
Yet Lily's quite unmeditated hex
would curse even a passionless pragmatic.
She couldn't help but make a warm impression,
and melted stone-faced Willy Storm's discretion.

Of course, there were those tiny purple shorts.
(She didn't expect that he'd arrive so early.)
"I was just playing at the tennis courts,"
Lil stammered, blushing like a guileless girly.
"So nice to meet a woman into sports,"
Will smiled, whistling through incisors pearly.
And, as she served him tea with cream and sugar,
Lil saw, by his swelling pupils, he really dug 'er.

Now if you think you know where this is going,
you've prob'ly been inspecting too much porn.
It's smart to do less telling and more showing,
but not to prematurely toot the horn.
Love's quill must not too quickly start a'flowing,
exhausting in a short and sudden storm.
(Though hesitation, too, can be a crime;
"Love at first sight," said Mae, "saves lots of time!")

And if you judge this a baroque attempt
to justify the ways of Lil to men,
whether you pardon, or hold her in contempt,
for kissing him once, then kissing him again,
Lil will remain, from human law, exempt.
For who is fit to call this love or sin?
God's mercy, and his wrath, are both preemptive;
we mortals ought, therefore, to live and let live.

By now, surely, the priggish have dropped out.
But who needs more than readers "fit though few?"
A kiss needs only two to give it clout;
vicarious eyes don't make a love more true,
nor do Byronic bards, messing about
with forced tropes that fools might misconstrue.
(Though some might argue love would not exist,
if poets' penurious pens did not persist!)

But neither Lil, nor Will, could care a fig
for keen voyeurs, or for myopic hacks
who kindle love, then snuff it like a cig.
Their love, like wild vines, grew through the cracks
of their own story. And neither cared to dig
too deeply to unearth the petty facts
they let stay buried, though they'd sometimes speak
of the curse of inherited wealth, and of Harrison Creek.

However, unlike Lil, Will wasn't estranged
from his own kin, though most found it awry
that, spite of wealth and school and stock exchange,
Will's dream of the simple life would never die,
and not a few considered it deranged
to spurn a trust to become a cable guy.
But what would *you* do? Isn't golf inane?
Wouldn't country clubs and plaid drive *you* insane?

Yes, William stormed with inner contradiction,
as Lil soon found. He worshipped *La Bohème*,
for instance. Mimi's tragical affliction
moved him as if she sang it just for him.
So Lily never dreamed she'd foster friction
by buying tickets for the both of them.
Will said he'd heard, but never seen an opera,
not *Tosca*, *Faust*, nor *Madame Lepidoptera*.

It would have been a first for Lily, too.
The closest that her little town had come
to such high glamour was when *Cats* passed through.
So now, though she'd, for weeks, eat like a bum,
and though her rent was almost overdue,
she thought two seats well worth the princely sum.
But love can't squeeze new pennies from old rock;
Lil fretted, now, how she'd afford a frock.

Lucky for Lily, *Fausto's Pawn and Loan*
was there to help (especially themselves).
She watched them rub the central scarlet stone
on her favorite filigree cross, like greedy elves.
"Don't worry, ma'am," they cooed, in unctuous tones.
"In six weeks time you'll find it on these shelves."
But Lily blanched to risk this talisman,
which shielded her heart better than any man.

That night, as William ordered, for the pair,
two plates of liver 'n onions from Kyle's Café,
he turned to see Lil waving in the air
the tickets she'd kept hidden all the day.
But, to her shock, Will answered with a stare,
his blue eyes freezing to a steely grey.
"Talking is pain," he said, invoking Rumi.
"I see, now, that you never really knew me.

"How could I stomach a bourgeois excursion
that Mimi, herself, could scarcely e'er afford?
Not even music muffles my aversion
for hypocrites who sob at every chord,
who trumpet a political conversion,
as long as serf stays serf, and lord stays lord,
who leave the balcony in tears, then yelp
imperious orders at their helpless help.

"Truth is I've seen *Bohème*, before, as well
as *Götterdämmerung*, and *Butterfly*,
and *Salomé*, and *Siegfried*, and *Seville*,
though surely you'll forgive my little lie.
A man should not be led, like this, to tell
shameful secrets he'd just as soon deny.
Did you really think that I had never been?
My parents are fuckin' sponsors, and I'm their kin!"

Lil gasped, and reached to clutch her treasured cross,
but Jesus, once again, was MIA.
Her eyes moistened like Mississipi moss,
and shed a single tear, which she let stay.
"I see how quickly you can choose to toss
my gift aside, but I will have my say—
money cannot buy poverty, dear Will;
a pauper's life is not some prince's thrill.

"For me, poverty's like a rabid bitch;
for you it's nothing but an affectation.
Beauty that would, the multitudes, bewitch,
you banish with a rationalization.
But neither would I care for being rich,
if it inspires such perverse privation.
And if you won't go with me to the show,
perhaps I should invite a different beau!

"'Love is the water of life'—so goes the spell
written by your favorite whirling Sufi.
Well maybe I should find a different well,
and you a guru who's not quite so goofy.
And while you're at it, why not junk that gel?
It makes your hair ridiculously poofy!"
Poor Lil was right, 'specially 'bout his hair.
A flock of seagulls nested in that lair!

And yet, regardless of her angry threat,
she sought no handsome substitute for Will.
But nor was plucky Lil about to let
a quarrel spoil her operatic thrill.
"Just look at that delectable coquette!"
one blade remarked, as Lil sat lone and still,
hoping that Will would show, and yet uncertain,
while staring, sadly, at the crimson curtain.

And sure enough, through mom's engraved binocular,
sly Will was there, espying his sweet pal,
and felt as if a jackal pierced his jugular,
when a stranger took the space beside his gal.
How could he know an inebriate avuncular,
having downed four shots to moisten his morale,
now groped to the seats he once had occupied,
ten lonely years ago, with his ex-bride?

Lil whispered, "Sorry but this seat's reserved,"
but maudlin drunks are not inclined to scram.
He mumbled in her ear, "You never lurved
me, darling," just as Mimi sang, "I am
tranquil and happy." Lil, though, was unnerved,
yet laughed at last, "Who really gives a damn?"
Her William Storm, that's who! And he was seething,
his mom astonished by his heavy breathing!

"Look at his fat head on her little shoulder,"
Will fumed. "She hasn't wasted any time!"
His mom guffawed, "You're dense as granite boulder!
That's not her date. I'll bet a Barber dime
that's cousin Bertha's harmless Uncle Holder.
It's said he was quite handsome in his prime,
but dwindled to a sad and drunken asshole,
after his frau forsook him for a basso."

Will vowed he'd win her back, or do his damndest,
so during break surprised her with his hand.
Lil rose, poor Holder's noggin slammed the armrest,
and then they laughed. "I know I can't demand
forgiveness," Will acknowledged, "for this tempest.
But now I place myself at your command,
and hope, if I achieve sufficient penance,
you'll have the mercy to suspend my sentence."

With that, he pulled out Lily's bartered cross,
and hung it gently round her tiny neck,
saying, "I never would have let you toss
your heart away, and don't ask how the heck
I ever found it." Lil was at a loss
for words, but not for smiles, and didn't object
when gazes turned to embraces, then to bussing,
despite the drunken Holder's grunts and cussing.

I'm sure you've guessed that, soon, a wedding followed,
in keeping with this tale's connubial themes.
And, oh the tears Lil's exes must have swallowed
when the Sunday rags' announcements mocked their dreams!
This was, of all her weddings, the most hallowed,
in a proper church, with proper nuptial memes.
Will brayed before the circumstance and pomp,
but Lily soothed him with a sexy romp.

Indeed, it was Will's mom who kept insisting
on marrying off her son in proper form.
Lil protested, but soon gave up resisting
what, surely, was, for wealthy folk, the norm.
And though Will's mom went far beyond assisting,
Lil found her almost temperate, for a Storm.
Truth is, Will's mom took rather well to Lil,
and Lil's own mom had left a chasm to fill.

The pair enjoyed a glorious honeymoon,
but after two enthralling weeks away,
strolling the sandy beaches of Cancun,
were happy to walk upon their native clay.
And though Will's father, with his silver spoon,
offered to buy 'em a home, in Horseshoe Bay,
they'd saved, instead, to buy a little cottage,
and wouldn't trade it for a sea of pottage.

But this is not a fairy tale, my friends.
Marriage can't turn a turnip to a rose.
Lil would have welcomed trying to make ends
meet, if her Will didn't always thumb his nose
at every steak, and force her to pretend
abiding loyalty to sloppy joes,
(to name just one of many long examples).
But let's dispense with further dull preambles—

She left him. Was it for *filet mignon*?
Amusing thought, though probably reductive.
And yet is food not the *sine qua non*
of love? Or is this reasoning not deductive?
Who cares? While Lil arranges her chignon,
and leaves her Will, with one last smile seductive,
I better run to catch a drink before
she meets, and mates, and marries number four.

Armando

His lover gone, the bed already made,
Armando idly gazed, through bamboo shade,
at the girl in the lot below checking her oil,
who held the dipstick, like a squeamish mohel,
far from her empire-waisted, tea-length frock,
while frowning at her frickin' engine block,
as spreading oil threatened her Mary Janes.
Armando slipped his slacks astride his Hanes,
and, like an angel, showed up just in time
to save those gorgeous shoes from the creeping grime
by lifting Lily gently to the curb,
as she struck his strapping chest and squealed "the nerve!"
Armando gestured to the oil that trailed
along the gutter, but Lil, still angry, railed,
"I'd rather ruin my shoes than die of fright!
Who do you think you are—some shining knight?
Now, if you please, I've got to get to work!"
Lily stomped off, exclaiming, "What a jerk!
And now there goes my bus. I'm so damn late!"
and, looking forlornly after it, pleaded, "wait!"
Just then Armando tapped her dainty arm,
"I only meant to save your shoes from harm."
"Are you insane?" she said, then slapped his face,
but he could only brighten at the grace
with which she arched her back and dealt that blow.
She reminded him of Audrey. No—Monroe,
or maybe *Kiss Me Kate*? No—*Lady Eve*.

She was like all, yet none he could conceive.
"I'll gladly take you anywhere you want,"
he offered, with inflection nonchalant.
"Alright," said Lil, "but don't get no ideas.
I work on Commerce at *Joe T. Garcia's*.
My shift just started. Please, let's make it snappy.
"No trouble, doll, just leave it all to Pappy!"
Armando smiled, showing off his dimple,
to Lily's glare. "OK, I'll keep it simple,"
he said, "and be a perfect gentleman!"
He dropped her off, went home, then downed some gin.

Next day, as she was waiting for a tow,
Armando gazed, again, at Lil below.
This time her Mary Janes were not in peril,
but while the tow truck man, with fit and feral
movements, mounted her Mustang firmly on
his waiting truck, Armando mused upon
how it must feel to be a tiny betty,
alone, and wanting, 'mongst a herd of heady
and lustful bucks, who'd certainly be gunning
to overwhelm her with sheer force, or cunning.
A girl like Lil must surely be on guard
'gainst every type of cad, or of canard.
She needed a Bogie, Mitchum, Dean, or Brando,

but most of all she needed an Armando!
And there was something 'bout this stylish shrew,
besides, though he could scarcely think it through—
Why was he aching, now, for this petite,
despite the twenty lovers at his feet?
Why would he, soon, spurn all his paramours
(well most of them), and dedicate his hours
to pining, plotting, and planning every word
he'd spin to snare the heart of this sweet bird?
A bird, no less, with neither wings nor wheels,
nor a mechanic willing to making deals—
in just four weeks, Lil needed to scrounge cash
for all the repairs. Meanwhile her morning dash
to the bus kicked off long days of waiting tables.
Lil's life soon mimicked all the fractured fables
her Aunt would wickedly tell, where Cinderella
couldn't get off work, so never found her fella'.

But, one day, while Lil waited at the stop,
Armando dropped by Elroy's auto shop,
where Lily's mustard Mustang was corralled.
"A final shine might rally her morale,"
Armand instructed, giving El a wink,
and then a cheque. "She's good to go, I think."
Armando parked th'emancipated 'stang

at *Joe Garcia's*, and prepped for the harangue
he knew he'd get, for pestering Lil at work,
There just was no dissuading this young Turk!
"What'll it be?" Lil asked, with cold inflection,
after Armando commandeered her section.
"Just you," he said, "and nothing less will do,
though if you have a twin, I'll take her too!"
"I'm not on the menu! Listen, my Don Juan,
I'm busy, see. I ain't got time for screwin'
around with bums who fetishize my shoes.
Now will it be tacos, tamales, tostada's, or booze?"
"I'll have the enchilada, green sauce please,
and beer, and, by the way, I like your knees!"
"Stop it!" Lil scolded, stomping to the kitchen,
but Mando thought her sass was pretty bitchin'!
Of course he craved sweet nothings from her too,
just not too many, lest they spoil the brew,
for love, though tender, yet requires a spark—
a minx, a cad, a driver in the dark.
Indeed, a car soon drove up for our hero,
so leaving a tip, he left in a Camaro.
"Good lord," Lil thought, "the fool forgot his keys."
But then she read his note — "Dear Lily, please
forgive me for that clumsy first encounter;
I didn't mean to seem like such a bounder.
Your car's outside, and purrs, now, like a cat—
a gift from me, and nothing more than that."

Lil dashed outside to tell Armando off.
"Who does he think he's foolin'?" Lily scoffed.
"Men fix your car, only to fix your wagon—
white knight one day, next day a drunken dragon."
But Lily's rage couldn't help but be undone
by her fresh-waxed Mustang, gleaming in the sun.

The two soon hung like Havilland and Flynn,
but, like them, stopped just short of that last sin,
until, one day, while dressed in fine attire,
Armand asked Lil to help him change his tire.
"Don't make me ruin my dress," protested Lily.
"Then take these gloves," he said, "my little filly,
and let me lay my jacket on the ground."
Lil smiled, kneeled, then trembled at what she found—
sitting next to the tire, a tiny box!
She opened it and squealed, "Armand, you fox!
Of course I'll be your faithful little Mrs.,"
then showered him with floods of squeaky kisses.
Armando took great pleasure in the planning.
He picked the gowns and even arranged the tanning.
It was a summer wedding after all;
who wants to show pale-cheeked to his own ball?
And Lil was glad to let him take the reins,
and touched by how her Mando took such pains,

even to find the best Stargazer Lilies;
clearly she was the heel of her Achilles.
Armando even nixed the bachelor party,
for a quiet night with pals, Elroy and Arty.
And after the honeymoon the fun kept goin'.
They watched old flicks, and sobbed to Leonard Cohen;
they salsa danced on sexy Saturdays;
their kitchen steamed, their satin sheets ablaze!
And Mando always helped with dish and mop,
and took the cars, with pleasure, to the shop,
saying, "I don't mind giving Elroy labor;
our Fords have never found a better neighbor!"
"You're right," Lil said, "you always think ahead.
What good's a chassis when the motor's dead?"

One day Lil thought she'd visit the garage,
to bring Armand and Elroy a barrage
of cookies, sandwiches, and Texas tea.
But Lil was ill-prepared for what she'd see—
Armando helping El hold up the walls,
staining his honor, and his coveralls!
I'll not get graphic, lest the censors yell,
but let's just say that Lil could clearly tell,
by the way Armand was probing Elroy's tailpipe,
he favored, not the female, but the male-type.

Lil pelted them with nuts and piston rings,
crying, "You've no idea how it stings
to catch you with this greasy, stain-clothed dick;
a married man's not s'posed to share his prick!"
Armando tried to make it up to her.
He bought her t-strapped heels and vintage fur,
a tasteful strand of graduated pearls,
and cameo earrings framed with antique curls.
But nothing he'd say, or do, or sacrifice
could ever win Armando back Lil's eyes,
and though his lovers were glad to lend a shoulder,
he never lost the ardent ache to hold her.
Poor Lily, too, could scarcely be consoled.
She tossed her Mary Janes, and even sold
her Mustang, with its bitter memories.
Nothing Armando touched could ever please
Lil any longer, though it was sad to lose
a man, at last, who loved to shop for shoes.

———————•◆•———————

All the Difference

A heart that's stuck in second gear,
and teeters between hope and fear,
may turn to God, or saint, or pope,
or even the daily horoscope.
So lovelorn Lil, fed up with Dios,
turned to Cosmo's advice for Leos—
New dudes won't help dashed hearts to mend;
turn not to man, but man's best friend.
"Why not?" thought Lil. "A doting dog
might see me through this dreary fog.
Dogs are loyal, unlike my spouses;
they don't need cash, or fancy houses.
They never yell; they never quibble;
they just want love, plus walks and kibble."
So Lil dashed to the local shelter,
where two sad mugs began to melt her—
a one eared German Shepherd, and
a tiny Chi, the color of sand.
Poor Lil knew she should pick just one,
thinking her nasty landlord, John,
might allow it, if he only saw the
scanty scat of a small Chihuahua.
Lil named her furry darling *Shorty*.
"He'll live," she thought, "'til I turn forty."
But Shorty moped while Lil was gone
working all night, from dusk 'til dawn,
at a dive bar, wearing a string bikini,

serving jello shots and stiff martinis.
"Screw John!" Lil cursed, returning to claim
her gentle giant, and, kissing his maimed
ear, she named her Shepherd *Hef*,
since he, though neutered, and somewhat deaf,
still liked to chase the young blonde bitches,
if only just to sniff their riches.

At last, Lil had a family.
"It's perfect", she smiled, "with just us three."
But John, like some Dickensian villain,
just seemed to have it out for Lil, and
sniffed for evidence 'round her yard,
gathering major and minor turd
to show her, barking, "Those mutts must go!
Don't bother begging. My no is no!
I told you once, the rules is rules!
Though luscious lips on precious jewels,"
John had to add, after checking out
poor Lily's tears and trembling pout,
"might convince me to change my mind!"
"Oh John!" Lil said, "you're awfully kind!
Come by my place tonight, at six;
I promise that you'll get your fix!"
And Lil was ready with John's reward

that evening, when he rang the door,
greeting him in a sheer silk nighty.
"John likes," he moaned, "good God almighty!"
"My pleasure," Lil said, gesturing *stay*
at her dogs, who eyed him like their prey.
"And don't mind them. Let's loosen your slacks!"
"Ok," John slobbered, "feel free to attack!"
Lil smiled, kneeled, then fondled his belt.
John grinned, grimaced, grunted, and yelped.
But, just as she licked his hirsute thigh,
Lil stopped, suggesting, "Let's first get high."
 "I like your style," John said. "Alright,
first toke, then tease, then tickle, then bite."
So he puffed, idly scratching his wankles,
while tighty whities hugged his ankles.
Lily inhaled, looked to her pets,
then calmly tapped three times on her chest.
Like lightning, Shorty leaped from the bed,
nipped John's nose, and peed on his head,
while Hef, as John shook Shorty loose,
clamped black jaws on his naked caboose,
'til the landlord howled, soiled the floor,
then stumbled, cursing, from Lily's door.

What matter that she'd have to move,
Now that our Lil got back her groove?

With Hef and Shorty at her side,
sad happenstance had better hide!
She'd find a cottage, with a yard,
her twin boys would be proud to guard,
with bonny bluebonnets blossoming wild,
far from traffic, or screaming child,
or sirens ringing, or neighbors yelling,
and naught but the sniff of canines smelling,
through long moist noses built for mutts,
flowers, and one another's butts.
Lil circled ads and drove around
for days, until at last she found
a cozy cottage on spacious acre,
and at a price that wouldn't break her!
But could she mow that giant lawn?
Lil had at least sufficient brawn
to carry heavy trays all night,
dodging drunks and ducking fights,
but could her callipygian ass
climb those endless hills of grass
with nothing but the tiny mower
her rugged landlord, Stuart, showed her?

Stu lived on the lot right next to Lil,
in an A-frame house, where, from the sill

one morn, he watched her struggle, cursing
the ancient mower, frowning and pursing
her lips as she forced it up the slope.
"She'll soon give up," he guessed, but nope,
she cut down every stubborn blade.
"I bet she'd love some lemonade,"
Stu thought, so quickly brought some over,
(dabbing his cheeks with musk and clover).
"Thirsty?" he asked. Lil grabbed the glass
and gulped, exclaiming, "You bet your ass!"
Stu frowned at the rusty hulk below her,
"I really should get a better mower!"
"No need," Lil said, "to find one finer;
it stalls a bit, but I'm no whiner."
"The carburetor might need a kit,"
wise Stu surmised. "Let's rest a bit,
then run to town and pick one up.
And you can bring along your pups.
We'll drop 'em off to get a groom;
I'll bring my boxer, Bud. There's room
in my old Ford." Lil nodded *yes*,
"Just let me wash and put on my dress."
When they got to Ernie's Auto Parts,
you could follow the trail of breaking hearts,
as every eye, in turn, spied Lil,
looking like April daffodil,

in yellow dress of eyelet and lace,
with hair pulled back from fresh-made face,
daintily dangling a little basket,
as Stu, beside her, inspected gaskets.
"The kit comes with those things already,"
said Lil, an ever helpful betty.
"That so?" said Stu, with grateful smile,
then added, "It might be a while
before they've groomed our three amigos;
why don't we snack some at Diego's?
They've got good tacos, great fajitas,
and awe-inspiring margaritas."
 "Yes," exclaimed Lil. "I'm ravenous!"
"How nice," Stu thought, "she doesn't fuss,
unlike so many of her sex,
'bout every calorie between decks."
Soon both, in cozy booth, were set,
laughing, and blushing, while they 'et,
but as eyes met, in pregnant pause,
Stu felt a pair of sharpened claws
clamp down, familiar, 'round his head,
and turned to see his ex, Big Red.
"Oh hell!" Stu winced, "not you, again!"
"Tsk, tsk," said Red, primping her mane,
in Lily's spoon, as make-shift mirror.
"Stifle it, Stu. You're not my Führer!

We're now divorced, have you forgotten?
Though I see your manners are still rotten;
you haven't introduced your date!
(She's cuter than that last one, Kate.)"
Lil smiled at Red's comedic nerve
and offered her a fat *hors d'oeuvre*.
"Don't mind if I do," responded Red,
then helped herself to the generous spread,
copping a seat right next to Lil.
"You mind?" she asked, taking a swill
from Lily's mammoth margarita.
"Thanks," she said, "my name's Anita,
but folks 'round here call me *Big Red*,
for my freckles, smile, and the flame on my head."
"It's nice to meet you, Red. I'm Lily.
I'm not Stu's date, but tenant, really,
and you can call me *Lil* for short."
"Okay, "Stu chimed, "can you transport
yourself to another table, now
that you've met my Lil and snaked our chow?"
"Why Stu!" Lil said, "that's awful rude.
Big Red is welcome to share our food."
"Don't worry," said Red, "my order's ready.
I'm taking it with me to meet my steady,
at Danny's Pub, in just a few.
Stop by, if you like, and have a brew.

It's just a couple blocks from here."
Red turned and smiled at Stu, "Bye Dear,"
then waved and blew a kiss at Lil.
Just then the waitress brought the bill,
asking, "Shall I add dessert to that?"
"No thanks," Stu sulked, "we've got to scat."
"Damn!" Lil thought, "what a thoughtless guy.
I could have devoured a slice of pie!"
"That Red," Stu scowled, "sees clear as mud.
To think we'd drink with her and her stud!"
And Stu went on to mope and frown,
all the long drive back in from town.

Next morn, as Lil was sipping tea
on her front porch, who did she see?
None other than the sheepish Stu,
with wild flowers wet with dew.
"I've come here to apologize.
I'm sorry you saw my mood capsize.
That Red was always a rogue torpedo,
sinking my spirit and my libido."
 "Thanks, Stu, they're beautiful," said Lil.
"I'm sure Big Red can be a pill,
but she didn't bother me one bit.
I like a woman who thinks her shit

don't stink. Besides, she's kind of fun."
Stu cracked, "Oh she's a son of a gun.
But that's the past; let's let it lie.
How 'bout I take you out for pie?"
"Oh Stu," Lil cooed, "I could hug your neck,
for being so sweet. Oh what the heck. . ."
She sighed, wrapping her tiny hands
around his collar. Her eyes' commands,
Stu's lips were happy to obey,
until an ass began to bray,
at least that's what Stu thought he heard,
not the raucous caw of a Scarlet bird!
"Hi y'all," Big Red saluted them,
"I just got done down at the gym,
and thought I'd tell Lil 'bout the sales
they're having on shoes at Bloomingdale's."
"Oh Red, that's very sweet of you,
Lil said, "but I've got plans with Stu."
"You heard," Stu scowled, "we're going out."
"Oh, to some fancy fishing route?"
Big Red shot back, then said,"Just joking."
Stu's face turned red, his ears 'gan smoking,
and he started to tell that Red what for
when, suddenly, through the porch screen door
and under their feet, a whirlwind passed.
'Twas Hef and Shorty, mighty gassed,

charging the black and white caboose
of Stu's cow Daisy, on the loose
in Lil's front yard, and madly mooing
to find two macho mutts pursuing,
the little one sniffing at her udder,
the big one snapping at her rudder!
Lil ran to grab her darlings' collars,
distracting them with hoots and hollers,
while Stuart tried to head off Daisy
before the canines drove her crazy.
But spite the bold pursuit serpentine
nothing could stop the stubborn Holstein,
'til, from her purse, Big Red withdrew
a Smith and Wesson 22,
freezing the action, at one try,
with a single shot into the sky.
Red smiled, "Best way to stop a male
from sniffing at your boobs and tail!"

That night, as Stuart lay in bed,
he cursed the day he met Big Red,
wondering what Lil was thinking, now,
after the chaos with ex and cow.
But Lil was still more charmed by Stu,
in fact, for how, his Daisy moo,

he gently kept from further harm,
leading her back to the warm barn.
Lil hoped to know this Stu much better,
but worried he might never let' er;
Stu didn't live like other men live,
being so quiet and so pensive,
like a modern Lone Star State Thoreau,
happily wat'ring his bean row,
patting his cow, and petting his dogs,
then reading by porch light, to the sound of frogs.
But Lily's worries were unfounded,
for Stu was not at all confounded
'bout his own feelings for Lil, and so
he asked her, first, to a picture show,
and then, the following night, to hear
the music sweetest to his ear,
a Bach concerto 'neath the stars.
"They say that men are all from Mars,"
Lil cooed, sipping on Stewart's wine,
"but you and Bach are both divine!"
A few days later, Stu sent daisies,
with a note that set her eyes all hazy.
"How did you know," Lil asked her Stu,
"it was my birthday?" "Come here you,"
Stu summoned, kissing her tender tears.
"I know that you have come to fear

that love is an insidious fog,
and marriage turns a prince to frog,
But seeing you, how could I frown?
How could I ever let you down?
Your smile to me's a perfect sonnet,
I love you Lil! I do, doggonit!"
So Lil spent day and evening lost
in Stu's warm arms, while he read Frost.

Alas, sometimes our common sense
is bought with sad experience—
your lover's ex, for goodness' sake
does not a bosom buddy make!
But Red was such a good ole gal,
Lil couldn't help but be her pal,
and didn't consider this a treason
since all could be made right through reason,
or so she thought. And so one day,
after long hours of lover's play,
Lil turned to ask her sated Stu,
"Big Red is always nice to you;
must you always be mean to her?"
"Lil, you'd coax a lion to purr,"
Stu smiled, "but Red could set a spittin',
howlin', and scratchin', a tiny kitten."

"Oh Stu! If hate were beer," said Lil,
"how many barrels would you fill?"
"Enough," Stu snapped, "it's not your business!
When can we stop this tedious quiz, Miss?"
"Sweet Stuart, now that you're my guy,
you're going to have to tell me why
you still despise Big Red so much!"
With that, Lily began to touch
Stu softly 'round his jaws and temples,
kissing his cheeks and charming his dimples.
Stu thought it most unfair how Lil
cajoled a helpless man to spill
his secrets, trapped in his own bed.
What had she done to his poor head?
To tell the truth, with little drilling,
love made his tongue both loose and willing.
"When I met Red, I was just fifteen,
a stammering boy in plaid and jeans.
Big Red was stacked, she smoked, she giggled
at all my stupid jokes. She jiggled
just where she should, but wasn't a tease,
easily giving herself to please
the one she loved, and always true
to me alone, and swore it too!
And since I thought, then, with my peen,
we hitched before we turned eighteen.

But before long, Red's voice grew gruff
and strident, nothing was enough—
not this broad stretch of country land,
nor the house I built with my own hands.
Her wanter was bigger than her getter;
I gave my best. She wanted better.
And when she took my best friend, Rudy,
I kicked her out on cheatin' booty!"
"Some women have big appetites,
but you're my only Mr. Right,"
soothed Lil. "You two were just mismatched,
but now you've hooked a better catch.
And I won't ever cheat on you,
I swear on Robert Frost, dear Stu.
But a girl still needs to have her friends
'cause, after all, she must depend
on women's advice, for many matters—
when hair's all wrong, and clothes in tatters—
and Red is fun, not one bit jealous.
Oh sure, she's loud and over-zealous,
she mouths a lot, and drinks a little,
but she's not rude, nor over-brittle,
and her heart's still bigger than her hair!"
"You're right. I guess I don't much care,"
Stu smiled, "now that I've found my heart,
if you share a laugh with that old tart,

as long as she don't jack my beer.
And thank God she ain't living here!"

Dear reader, I've something to confess,
and please don't think of me the less.
Since stories are such hard taskmasters,
we writers dally with disasters,
but this Big Red's a big red herring!
Indeed, Red proved to be a caring
friend, to Lily, and to Stu,
though sometimes she purloined his brew,
and yes, was disappointed by
Lily's decision to defy
tradition, and, with Stu, elope,
despite Red's *maid of honor* hope.
Big Red loved taffeta, after all,
organza, and a gaudy ball,
so, on return as Man and Mrs.,
the lovers were met by balloons and kisses,
by splendid cake, and laughter hearty,
'cause Red surprised them with a party!
And though Lil's Stu was number five,
he proved the aptest man alive
to love his Lil in every way.
If only Lil could make time stay,

and will away the thieves of love,
the things one pales to be thinking of,
especially when a love is young—
I can barely force my pen, or tongue,
to say what stole Lil's darling from her—
it was that slut that we call *cancer*.

Lil buried Stu with his Robert Frost.
"Over all, is the highway dust,"
Lil said to Red, both dressed in black.
"I'll never have my Stuart back,
but I was his true beloved, once,
and that makes all the difference."

———◆———

Love Was a Need

Our Lily wed four toads to find one prince,
and then he had to go and die on her.
Poor Lil would never find a way to rinse
that last one from her locks. No one could stir
and comfort her, at once, like her last sir.
But Lily was too young to just concede.
For her love was no game, love was a need.

But for Juan Jardinero, it was both.
And when he eyed our Lily, all alone,
wand'ring the riverwalk, he bowed, "I'm loath
to see such beauty, sad, in San Antone;
why don't you smile, and throw a man a bone?"
"Do I know you, Sir?" Lil asked the blue-eyed flirt.
"Or do you seek to score with some new skirt?"

"I've never seen a skirt more pretty than
your own," Juan flattered, "and I'm no common Joe!"
"I'll tell you this just once—I have a man!"
Lil lied, rememb'ring her departed beau,
"but now he's gone!" She cried, and turned to blow
her tiny nose into a pink lace hanky,
diverting suave Juan's hopes for evening panky.

"There, there," he soothed, trying to coddle Lily.
"Get your hands off me, you freak!" She pulled away.
"I'm trying to comfort you," Juan countered, "really!"
"Oh that's just what a creep like you would say,"
Lil cried, aiming her can of pepper spray.
Oh why do damsels' tears invite seduction?
(Although for craftier dames that's crying's function!)

Lil fired at point blank range into Juan's face,
but his relentless eyes refused to tear.
She fumbled, cursing her skinny can of mace,
and tried to fire again as Juan loomed near.
But he grasped her wrist and whispered, "Have no fear!
Tonight you'll dine with Juan, on the veranda,
then kiss his parted lips when he commands ya."

Lil's knees went weak. Juan quickly caught her fall,
carrying her to a sweetheart bench nearby.
"I'm fine," Lil said, "I need to eat, that's all."
"I know I'm just a stranger," Juan said, "but why
not dine with me tonight? Please don't be shy."
Soon Lil was scarfing catfish and lemonade,
while Juan nibbled, dreaming of getting laid.

Lil woke up in Juan's arms, but couldn't remember
just what had brought her there, the night before.
And yet, she had no wish to 'scape the tender
embraces of her charming paramour.
And, to be blunt, she felt a little sore
when, swinging her legs, she tried to leave the bed.
Better to settle back and give Juan head.

Lil rose again, at sunset, all alone,
wondering what had happened to her Juan,
and fearing that the words on her dead love's stone
couldn't reconcile with what she just had done—
it had only been ten months since Stu'd been gone,
and here she was, fresh-fucked by some fair stranger.
(How can I help but end this line with *danger*?)

But soon Lil's guilt was drowned by hunger pangs,
so she went to rifle Juan's refrigerator.
"There's nothing but red wine and liver. Dang!"
Lil cried, "I'd settle for a cold potater!
Can't wait for Juan. I'll catch up with him later."
But as she left to grab some dogs and cheetos,
Juan drove up, with a mess of hot taquitos.

"Oh Juan, I'm famished. How'd you read my mind?"
"I know you, Lil, I've known you all my life.
And I will love you 'til the stars unwind!
"But Juan," Lil said, "I'm someone else's wife,
in my soul, still." "But Lil, your is heart is ripe
again. You can't sow beauty in decay.
And I'll not let you waste your love away."

Juan swore, again, he'd never let her go.
And Lil couldn't help but pledge eternal passion,
though adding, "Juan, you really cannot know
when jealous Death, our hopes, might come a dashin'."
"Death swung at me once," Juan smiled, "I returned the blow,
and beat Death's ass until, from two black eyes,
he wept like a bitch, and then I stole his dice."

"I reckon you romanticize that brawl.
My Stu had no such power over death.
The reaper will democratize us all,
in our nineteenth year or in our ninetieth.
One day he'll come to steal my own last breath.
But we, the living, must do what the living do,
and now I'd love to share this meal with you."

"I'm sorry," Juan said, "I ate while I was out.
I'll shower. Why don't you eat and watch the tv?"
Lil scanned the news, but soon began to shout,
"Oh no! Juan come and see; it's Pastor Peavey!
They found him pale and cold beneath the levee.
Ten pints of blood appear to have been drained.
How that was done has yet to be explained."

"That's one less charlatan," Juan sneered, "Who cares?
These men of God are all about the cash,
and gulling the public with their pious airs.
Good riddance to the snake-oil-peddling trash!
I pray they burn his canting corpse to ash!"
Lil reached to clutch her cross, as Juan snarled on,
then shrieked when she discovered it was gone!

Casually, Juan remarked, "It's in my drawer.
The chain broke off when we made love last night."
"Why did I fail to notice that before?"
Lil asked, "I never let it leave my sight."
"The jeweler will soon set it aright,"
Juan soothed, kissing our Lily's naked neck,
then leading her to his moon-soaked wooden deck.

After many amorous nights and dream-filled days,
Juan asked if Lil would spend her life with him.
She answered, calmly, "yes", though a strange haze
would cast her wedding skies uncanny dim,
and the JP's office seemed unseemly grim,
and Juan's cold eyes ne'er glowed so bright and blue,
as when the justice pledged them to be true.

"I could have asked for an eternity,"
Juan bragged, "but love is truer when it's mortal."
"Oh Juan," Lil scoffed, "the things you say to me!"
She smiled and asked him, with a teasing chortle,
"Will you be Heathcliff, scratching at my portal?"
Juan laughed. "This night will never dim," he said,
"and no man ever snatch you from my bed."

From that day on, their households were united.
Juan bonded, too, with Lily's furry friends.
Lil loved to see her hungry guys excited
when he brought home, from the butcher, odds and ends.
'Course like all couples they fought, then made amends,
'bout little things, like garlic in the sauce,
or whether Christ was false as Santa Claus.

But Juan's nocturnal schedule soon got old.
He wrote cheap horror fiction for his pay,
and, claiming the night would make his pen more bold,
slept with black curtains drawn throughout the day,
while Lil was off, while sun shone, making hay.
Lil did make time for naps, some afternoons,
so they'd still have some chance to make like spoons.

But noontime nookie only went so far
to pardon all those undone honey-dos—
Juan grudged to change the oil in either car,
replace old bulbs, or tighten loosened screws,
and really gave poor Lil the housewife blues
when he ignored her desperate pleas emphatic
to exterminate the bats, up in the attic.

What worried Lil the most was how, at night,
Juan insisted the windows be left open.
He said the whispering breezes helped him write,
but Lil exclaimed, "Are you really such a dope? And
have you forgot the reason for my fright—
the killer who starred, again, in last night's news?
They found that pedo priest, dead in the pews,

"and last week found that right wing politician,
who took those bribes, dead as a lump of dough,
just after they found that vegan esthetician,
cold beside his face-lifted marketing ho."
"Don't fret," said Juan, "you're safe in our chateau.
I hear your every breath, your every peep,
and keep a vigilant eye over your sleep."

Such sentiments might once have seemed romantic,
but now Lil found them strange, and rather cheesy.
The thought of more such drivel made her frantic,
though thoughts of hurting Juan made her feel queasy,
so she tried her best to break it to him easy—
"It's me, not you. Your love has been infallible!
It's just that we're a little incompatible."

Juan's eyes grew wide, and shot with maddened hues.
Incisors broke beyond his trembling lips.
But, pulling back, he said, "I cannot use
this power. My lust for you is far eclipsed
by love, which lies beyond all spell or ruse.
Your loss will be an everlasting bruise
upon my soul, if I've one left at all.
But I will never silence your heart's true call."

Paul Simon sang of break-ups just like this—
One likes the windows open, the other closed.
Lil had been blinded by immortal kiss,
and Juan believed their love was presupposed.
But now both fantasies had been exposed.
Still, what is love if you don't risk your neck?
Though, if it last, both hearts must stay on deck.

As California Sun

With six loves lost, and worn, but eager, heart,
our Lil packed bags, and mutts, for California,
like many a girl who dreams of a fresh start.

And at the risk this story might be borin' ya,
I'll let on now—our Lil remains disposed
to marry again. Don't say I didn't warn ya!

So read on friends! Tidbits will be disclosed
in *terza rima*, for your entertainment,
(and, also, for my own, you may suppose!)

You well might wonder where poor Lily's pain went,
but she was dogged as California sun,
and, when it came to love, didn't know what *sane* meant.

For now, though, Lil just wanted to have fun
disporting with her pooches by the shore,
before her Shepherd Hef's dog years were done.

Lil's hounds had never strolled the strand before,
but, when the tide tickled their furry feet,
it seemed that they could want for nothing more!

Now, San Diego's beaches were all sweet,
but Lily thought a place just steps from sand,
in wondrous Windansea, could not be beat.

'Course coastal digs are always in demand—
a shabby cottage, with a tiny yard,
was all Lil's Texas dollars could command,

and for her neighbor, an unshaven bard
who sang, and strummed, and chanted all night long—
the Belgian scholar, Monsieur Jacques Bâtard—

not to mention his twenty-four-hour throng
of student groupies, coming and a going,
often in scarcely more than bra or thong!

And after weeks awake, from this cock's crowing,
Lil rapped, at last, the scholarly satyr's door,
trying to mask the anger that had been growing.

Bâtard assumed it was the sophomore
who'd promised to come by that day, at one,
and sprang to the door, expecting an easy score.

"At the risk of interfering with your fun,
good sir," Lil sassed, "you've kept me up for weeks.
If you don't keep it down, I'll come undone!"

But Jacques, dumbfounded by her rosy cheeks,
her pleading ardor, and her soft brown eyes,
could scarcely bring his arrogant lips to speak.

"Please answer me!" Lil pleaded, until her cries
melted the heart even of this jaded cad,
(with help from décolletage, and creamy thighs!)

Jacques smiled, promised, but then felt strangely sad.
Next night, instead of hos, he studies Keats,
and the next night too, and next. Was he going mad?

Why did the thought of coeds 'neath his sheets,
which once amused him, now give him the blues?
What happened to his taste for vulgar sweets?

"How can this be?" Jacques marveled. "I've got to lose
this mad obsession with that sleepless beauty.
Lucky, I'm off to lecture in Santa Cruz!"

But Jacques could run as far as Timbuktuty;
it wouldn't make a jot of difference.
Desire far outranks professional duty!

Though love had not completely sacked his sense;
yes, he forgot his lecture notes on Chaucer,
but made good use of a peer's concupiscence—

a feminist scholar, who fancied bucks who bossed her.
"I'll type your notes," she said, "if you spank my ass,
then make me lap, like a dog, from a China saucer."

Strangely, this simple request now seemed so crass!
But Jacques did need the help preparing slides,
so he complied, for the sake of next day's class.

Indeed his lecture, peppered with witty asides,
was a great success, and basking in applause,
Jacques whispered to himself, "The dude abides,"

even while pretty scholars, with groping claws,
fondled his arm, and tempted with breasts and buns,
hoping to lure a genius to their jaws.

And yet they might as well have been old nuns,
or aging actors hamming it up in drag,
or female truckers hauling several tons,

for, without trying, Lil had fixed her flag
in Jacques' cold heart, once barren as the moon.
Now she alone, it seemed, was worth a shag!

Lil, however, danced to a different tune,
shunning her lovesick neighbor at every turn,
(though happy he'd shut down his sex saloon!)

It seemed to Jacques, not even Yeats could yearn,
like this, for the indomitable Maude Gonne.
His own heart was a second Troy to burn!

At least, he was no triple fool, like Donne—
he loved, but hadn't whined his love in poems.
But wait! A sonnet just might sway this swan!—

The Confession

I'd always thought, before I'd seen your own
that eyes of blue or green would vanquish brown.

Please tell how I, that error, might atone,
before you slam stern judgment's gavel down.
For had I not confessed this sin to you,
this prideful prejudice against all eyes
of neither verdant, nor of azure, hue,
I'd seem, to you, only a man who lies.
And now that courtliness has tipped my hand,
it's not just chocolate eyes that summon me.
But neither do I dare to make demands.
of your hard heart, from mine of ripened brie.
I only hope you'll, someday, be my femme.
And as for blue-eyed sluts? To hell with them!

Jacques hopped the little gate between their homes,
clutching the clever poem he'd just dashed off,
as well as, for her pooches, three fat bones.

"And what brings *you* here?" Lily quizzed the prof.
"I come with verse," he smiled, "and canine treats."
Lily restrained her righteous urge to scoff,

and soothed her riled up dogs, "Pipe down my sweets!"
then calmly accepted poem, plus bones, from Jacques,
saying, "I'll read this while they scarf their eats."

Lil shut the door, secured the dead bolt lock,
then scanned Jacques' verse, which instantly recalled
a poem once writ to her by some dull jock—

a scheming young lothario who scrawled
the self-same poem to twenty separate chicks,
who, disabused, were suitably appalled.

"These types," Lil thought," know plenty 'bout their dicks;
but what they don't know dick about is women!
To them, love's but a ruse to get their kicks.

"He'd have more luck importing a bride from Yemen
than winning me. Who does he think he is?
I'm sure he's most in love with his own semen."

And yet, though Jacques was proud to be a wiz
at heartless wooing, 'twas love indeed, at last,
that drove him to save, for Lil alone, his jizz.

Still, how long could he lump this endless fast?
Lil's heart, for many months, appeared impenetrable.
Was Jacques, spite all his conquests, yet outclassed?

Jacques found such doubts absurd, indeed, untenable,
He was the very model of ladies man!
Surely, in time, his Lil would grow amenable,

and, hopefully, before the copper tan
and potent pecs of the dude next door could play
upon her heart, and turn her from her man.

(Course, if Jacques knew that surfer was quite gay,
he might have spared himself much consternation,
and months of doubt about his own cachet!)

At last, one day, Jacques' wistful meditation
was broke by passionate pounding on his door.
'Twas Lil in tears, and hopeless desperation—

"It's Hef! Come quick!" cried Lil. "He's on the floor
inside, passed out! Please help him to my jeep.
I hope it's just some fit, and nothing more!"

But Jacques soon knew that this was Hef's last sleep.
His pulse was mute. His noble heart had quit.
Jacques broke it gently. Lil began to weep,

"No please! He can't be gone! This can't be it!
Just yesterday, he gamboled on the sand.
And now I cart his carcass to the vet?"

"I'll take it there," Jacques cradled Lily's hand.
"Please let me do that for you. Know, at least,
I'm here for you. I hope you understand."

It broke Jacques' heart to see his Lil so *triste*.
He couldn't confess his love, just yet, but vowed
to ease the death of her beloved beast.

With songs, and pranks, and poetry Jacques ploughed
through Lily's grief all winter's long abyss,
hoping that from the sadness where he sowed

such sweetness, there might grow new bliss.
And then, one April morning, Lil returned
from a long walk, with flowers, and a kiss.

"Oh Lil! You've no idea how I've yearned
for you. Nor how far I have now evolved
from my old self. And have you also burned?"

Lil nodded, and Jacques felt himself absolved
from all the perfidies of former days.
And as they grew still closer, Jacques resolved,

this time, to do just what his conscience says,
letting it guide him through the fiery truths
of love, that Lil might be his only miz.

Indeed, Jacques gladly curbed the riot of youth,
and cleaved to Lil as his eternal bride,
taking to marriage like gin to sweet vermouth.

And Jacques was a model husband. I mean aside
from, now and then, a shapely noon martini.
"Sweet Lil will never know," he thought. "Besides,

"a silky slattern in a sheer bikini
can't always be resisted, 'less you're loopy.
And it means nothing! Lil is my true queenie!"

And it's not as if he groped at every groupie.
He was home with Lily almost every night,
and making love, not simply making whoopee!

He really loved her, tried to treat her right,
lavished her with lattes and sticky buns,
defending her from even the subtlest slight.

But a married man who uses up, then shuns,
so many bimbos, meets a bunny boiler
at last, and it need only take just one.

Indeed, before Jacques had a chance to foil her,
some loony left a note on Lily's sill
that proved a most efficient marriage spoiler.

Though, this time, I've scarce sympathy for Lil.
To thwart these twists of plot Shakespearean,
only a man of honor fits the bill.

And willful blindness is a kind of sin.
It's one thing when your prince turns out a cad.
It's quite another to know that going in.

Lil shared, herself, the blame for being had.

Evergreen Lil

Attention, oh loyal subscriber to tales of
   personal triumph—
like a bathtub whiskey imbiber, the laugh is on
      your, not on *my* rump.
'Cause this story's a true picaresque, not a saga of
      personal growth.
It won't prove a great Oprah success, nor appear on
      her show coast to coast.
And though many might sell their own soul to
      smooch with a woman so fetching,
though Faustian kisses cajole many maids to wake
      up as sad Gretchens,
though Lil wept as oft as young Werther, and was
      virginal peasantry purty,
you won't see here a tragic self-murder, as you
      would in the dramas of Goethe.
No, Lil, who went through seven misters in
      eighteen short years, remained sweet.
She was free of the blistering bitters of wives too
      dull to retreat.
Thou hast conquered, oh evergreen Lil, through six
      struggles with marital stress,
and emerged, with an unbowed will, from one dear
      beloved's sad death!
Of course, I, who've endured each romance at a
      distance, vicariously,

if not for a hoped for advance, would have quit 'ere
the count got to three.
Now I know that you might find it crass that I'm
writing for coin, about Lil,
who, herself, couldn't care less about cash. But one
needs a scribbling shill,
like Shakespeare, Dante, or me, to bring fame to a
lovelorn fool.
But if only poor Lil would agree to pan gold from
some old coot's drool!
Are you shocked, dear readers, I'd whore my own
heroine, for some quick bucks?
If I wouldn't, you'd think me a bore, now wouldn't
you? Hypocrite fucks!

Now, Lil stayed remarkably chill on the respites
between her spouses,
and lovers prove less of a pill while they stay in
their separate houses,
but, at last, one must choose to get hitched or to
split. Of course, you know some
will begin like princes bewitched, then devolve into
pond-choking scum.
You might date them for kicks, for a spell, then cast
them right back to the sea,

but some can propose so damn well that a girl just
    has to say *"oui!"*
And how many times had some charmer busted our
    Lil's pretty balls?
At this point, the one to disarm her best come with
    no magic, at all!
She didn't fancy a smooth talking dandy, but
    someone who'd grow on her slowly,
someone more than enchanting eye candy (though,
    of course, not especially homely!)
And, this time, Lil solemnly promised she'd *not* be
    the innocent prey.
No, she'd be the pitiless huntress, and search for a
    sweetheart to slay!
There's a time, her shrewd grammy once said, when
    it's prudent to turn the tortilla.
How hard could it be? Men are bred so they'd
    much rather screw ya than flee ya!

For the very first time in her life, Lil was hatching
    an amorous plan.
But where could a would-be sweet wife find a
    modest, reliable man?
Best avoid arriviste cocktail lounges, like *Jack's, La
    Valencia* or *George's,*

where the rich, married coot often scrounges, and
    the middle-aged gold-digger gorges.
And don't *ever* set foot through the treacherous
    doors of the neighborhood churches,
lest greedy, self-righteous, and lecherous hypocrites
    spoil your searches.
So Lil scoured the everyday places— *Sam's
    Hardware*, and *Lou's Fluff and Fold*,
and she scanned all the promising faces that
    Pannikin's Coffee could hold.
She searched *Busy Bee* and *The Shack*, and she
    browsed through *D. G. Wills Books*,
while always parading her rack, and practicing
    "come-hither" looks.
And, indeed, Lil soon netted her prey— a man who
    loved working with numbers,
a patient and mild CPA who seemed in no hurry to
    hump 'er.
After seventeen dates, Lily fretted Chuck might
    never make the first move,
but a week in Big Sur at last whetted his hunger to
    get in the groove.
Now his kiss didn't quite make Lil see stars, and his
    telescope wasn't a Hubble,
but then Chuck stayed away from dive bars, and he
    loathed disagreements and trouble.

He was less of a dashing young Rhett than a shy,
      unassuming, sweet Ashley,
but then Lil was no greedy Scarlett, just looking for
      thrills, and for cash, see?
Why must love have a fiery sting? Lily needed a
      calm, steady flame,
so when Charlie, at last, bought a ring, she said,
      "Yes! I will take your last name!"

Lily's wedding and honeymoon, both, went
      smoothly, with nary a glitch,
and, for many months after their troth, Lily found
      few occasions to bitch.
At seven a.m. sharp, Chuck would kiss her, before
      driving off to his job,
and each night, around ten, he'd caress her, not just
      when his johnson would throb.
On Saturdays they'd see the flicks, and always to
      dinner on Friday.
On Sundays they'd help his mom fix up her house,
      keeping things nice and tidy.
But in time this routine became banal; Lil craved
      something different and new,
and, dear readers, I do not mean *anal*, you carnal,
      concupiscent crew!—

but a hot air balloon for the pair, with champagne,
    over dazzling Del Mar.
Just perhaps, Charlie's kiss, in midair, might, at last,
    help our Lily see stars.
And, indeed, she'd not seen him so pert, so aroused
    and enraptured, before;
Chuck queried the pilot 'bout skirt, about burners,
    and ballast and gore—
"Do you carry much propane to spare? And is this a
    double lapped seam?
How much weight can this gondola bear? And
    what is the maint'nance routine?"
"Here you go," hopeful Lily broke in. "Let's savor
    some bubbly, my dear."
Chuck sipped, and then smiled, and, then, quizzed
    again the bemused gondolier.
Poor Lil turned her thoughts from her lover,
    proceeding to get rather tipsy,
'til Charlie was shocked to discover Lil dancing,
    alone, like a gypsy.
So much for a glorious thrill, for a break from the
    usual diversions!
And, after the hangover, Lil lost her faith in
    romantic excursions.
But perhaps Chuck would like to read poetry!
    "Edna St. Vincent Millay,"

said Lily one night, "writes so quotably 'bout all her
    rolls in the hay."
Chuck nodded, "Oh yes. Very true," then went
    back to his New York Times.
"And what," Lil persisted, "would *you* say 'bout
    Edna Millay's use of rhyme?"
"Oh just fine," Charlie said, as he smiled, and
    sipped from his company mug.
"Want a refill?" Lil asked, halfway riled. Chuck said
    "sure," giving her a quick hug.

Lily felt rather blue all through May, and these
    feelings of impending doom
only grew with the deepening grey that followed,
    here known as *June Gloom.*
Then one day, while, at *Warwicks*, Lil scanned for a
    book that might strengthen her spirit,
she noticed a lecture was planned for four, and she
    might as well hear it.
Simon Schama, the noted historian, was peddling
    his new publication—
*From the Vikings to the Victorians: a Tale of the
Albion Nation.*
Lil adored both the speech, and the speaker, and as
    he was signing her book,

Simon smiled at the signature seeker, "Know a
	place with a talented cook?"
"I love *Wahoo's Fish Taco*," Lil lauded, "it's fun, and
	it's so economical!"
Simon grinned, and her prudence applauded; 'twas
	sweet, and a little bit comical.
"Don't worry 'bout price," he replied, "and if *you*
	say it's good, then it is!"
"Never let it be said that I've lied," Lily joked, "to a
	history wiz!"
"And will it be said you objected," he winked, "to
	come for a bite?"
"My husband's at work," Lil reflected, "'til six, so I
	guess it's alright."
"And you must," Simon said, "recommend the
	tastiest treat on the menu."
And in truth, Lil found food and new friend fine as
	any at fancier venue!
Chowing down on char-grilled mahi tacos with
	black beans and rice, how they talked
about all from Plantagenet wackos to Orwell and
	then Johnny Locke!
But when Simon asked Lil up above to his room,
	she politely declined;
Lily felt she'd already made love with her eager and
	ravenous mind.

Simon walked Lily back to her car, where he stole
    one long, lingering kiss,
and Lil knew, as he waved from afar, things at
    home were sorely amiss.

Now Chuck was no simpleton, either; he just
    focused on practical things.
He well knew that his Lily was eager to spread
    intellectual wings.
She went off, when she could, to night lectures at
    State, or at UCSD,
and Charlie admired his go-getter, and couldn't care
    less 'bout the fees.
But Lil wished she could talk about things with
    Chuck, like she chattered to Schama,
about fools, and villains, and kings, about lyric, and
    epic, and drama.
And though Lil couldn't get Simon's kiss, both
    gentle and strong, off her mind;
she could do nothing *but* reminisce— Charles
    wasn't the passionate kind.
"There's something I'm missing," Lil sobbed, one
    morning, quite out of the blue.
"You mean," Charlie asked, "we've been robbed?
    Has someone stole something from you?"

"I hoped that in time," Lily grieved, "we would
    blossom in ardor and zeal.
But I've tried, and I just can't believe that is what
    either one of us feel.
And *you*, Charlie, isn't it true, you're just going
    through the motions yourself?
What you're feeling for me, wouldn't you feel the
    same, with somebody else?
"You couldn't be more wrong about me if you
    tried!" Chuck lamented. "Lil, sweety,
could it be, like my colleagues for fee, for the drug
    of romance you're too greedy?
For myself, it had never seemed fated to *find* a love,
    much less get hitched;
for forty long years, I have waited for *you*, and now
    I get ditched?
Are you saying that I'm too phlegmatic? That you
    crave one more boyishly buoyant?
An uxorious, fawning dramatic, or foppish,
    philand'ring flamboyant?
Can I sway your hungering heart? I fear it will do as
    it bosses.
I love you. But, if we must part, say it now, Lil, and
    I'll cut my losses."

Were Lil's hopes so deformed by the sham desires of
    so many *pendejos*
that she couldn't see the good in the man who
    stood firm, before her own *ojos*?
Lil regretted, at once, all the painful, unmerited
    words she'd just said.
(And your narrator, too, feels disdainful, and
    cannot forgive her, just yet!)
She stayed, for a while, but her Charlie could never
    quite love her the same.
And Lily, this time, could really find none, but her
    own self, to blame.
Then again, why should Lil be a settler for someone
    whose kiss didn't thrill her?
Instead of that fate, far, far better for Lil, that this
    narrator kill her!

———◆———

Happy Either Way

L il wasn't the type to marry well,
     and then divorce a whole lot better.
She was no profligate jet setter,
throwing her cash around pell-mell.

Of course, she got small settlements,
but had no wish to ask for more,
and, from the time she was dirt poor,
Lil handled money with good sense.

And now, with bonds, CD's, and stocks,
plus part time work at selling books—
long as she shunned those realtor crooks—
Lil needn't fear financial shocks.

She hadn't played as safe at love!
Eight mates she'd loved and lost, plus dogs,
though made her way through heartbreak's fogs
to the clear air, with fresh resolve.

And had Lil's heart, at last, grown sage?
Could she distinguish cad from prince?
Had she transcended innocence,
despite a face which showed no age?

Lil welcomed floods of suitors, when
she was but young, and gullible,
earnest, wide-eyed, and bountiful,
a lamb just barely out the pen.

And, still, grown men, and young bucks, too,
flocked to our Lil in every season,
though many, finding her wit a treason,
called her a *witch,* and soon withdrew.

But, now, Lil welcomed having space
to read, to think, to make good friends,
to, with her mother, make amends
at last, kissing her tear-strewn face.

"I'm sorry, daughter. I turned on you,
but you were right. Tom was a crook.
For lying son, your mom forsook
her only daughter, for being true."

It'd been Lil's dream to walk the sands
of California with her mom,
and now, forgiving palm in palm,
they strolled the San Diego strands.

Lil wished her mother could stay near,
but Mom was used to Harrison Creek,
and so Lil phoned throughout the week,
and flew to see her twice a year.

Lil also met a new friend, Lola,
who'd moved from some place really cold,
exactly where, she never told,
until one night, o'er rye and cola—

"I left a man in Winnipeg
who cheated with a two-bit ho,"
she said. "He pleaded, 'please don't go,'
but I didn't stay to hear him beg."

"I've been there," Lil commiserated.
"If they cheat once, they'll cheat again,
and whoring is man's favorite sin.
I'm thinking love is overrated."

"Now don't go getting bitter, Lil.
It makes you old and you're too pretty.
I didn't move to this fair city
to sulk," she said, then took a swill.

"Dance with me, now," said Lola, standing.
"But there's no dance floor in this bar,"
protested Lil. "Why do you care?"
asked Lola, in a tone commanding.

And, as they danced beside their stools,
men started sending over drinks.
Lo winked at Lil and said, "Methinks
men, everywhere, are cunt-struck fools."

"But I can't drink all those!" Lil frowned.
"Just pass them over here, girl scout,"
a voice from two stools down cried out,
belonging to a busty blonde.

"I'm Ricki," she said, and moved in closer.
"I'm Lil, and here's my good friend, Lola."
"Pleased to meet you, and good to know ya."
"Go 'head, sit down," Lo said, "it's kosher."

"We partying, girls, or drowning sorrows?"
Miss Ricki probed, "Not that it matters.
When ain't my poor heart all in tatters,
yet hoping, still, for bright tomorrows?"

That Ricki seemed one special dame,
and Lo had loads of charm, as well.
Why do men hurt such dazzling belles?
Why do they treat love like a game?

The three girls pondered, through their gin,
the mysteries of the male agender,
then, for a fun, though fruitless, bender,
four days later, they met again.

Soon, weekly, Lil, with Rick and Lo,
were chilling at *Forever Fondue*,
and, life now smooth, Lil 'gan to rue
her many years of marital woe.

She liked her peaceful dawns, alone,
stretching her limbs free on the bed,
without love's troubles in her head,
nor, 'tween her thighs, some morning bone.

She sipped her joe at *Pannikin*,
reading her Tolstoy and Kundera,
and noted, women of every era
endured, from men, identical sin.

But Lily couldn't condemn all men,
when she'd, herself, done Charlie wrong,
and dear, dead Stu was kind and strong.
She still could fall in love again.

Lil would be happy either way.
But better, indeed, to be alone,
than drown in bad testosterone,
as Lily's mother liked to say.

Lucky, Lil's books and broad brimmed hat
kept out the shallow interlopers,
those witless, bimbo-chasing gropers
looking to pet some pussycat.

"Anna Karenina's one great book,"
a voice called out to Lil, one day.
"Sure is," Lil barked, "now go away!"
then caught the man's downfallen look.

"I'm sorry," Lil apologized,
"that Vronsky made me lose my temper;
you just got caught in my distemper.
This Tolstoy has me hypnotized!"

"That's certainly forgivable.
He has the same effect on me.
Kundera might say we're kindred, he
thought common books meant common soul."

"I've read Kundera's *Lightness of Being*,"
Lil said. "The hero was quite conceited,
flip about sex, and always cheated.
That's not a story I plan re-seeing."

"Well, I can't say I blame you there.
And by the way, my name is Martin,"
he said. "I hope that we aren't startin'
on the wrong foot; let's clear the air."

"And what would we be starting, sir?
You seem presumptuous as Vronsky.
I'm not Anna, don't fixate on me.
I'm not as fond of trains as her."

Then Martin laughed, and asked her name,
bought Lil some tea, and nabbed her number,
lest chances lost disturb his slumber.
He felt he'd met his destined dame.

But that's exactly what Jake Green thought,
when he met Lil at farmer's market,
and then, again, one day at *Target*.
Could she be who his heart, and peen, sought?

Jake had just won the Pushcart Prize,
for poems denouncing ersatz bards,
smashing them to sad heaps of shards.
Jake lived to sneer and satirize.

And while Lil shopped for hose and socks,
Jake seized the opportunity,
before his precious hind could flee
to dressing room, to try on frocks.

"What's your opinion, Miss?" he asked.
"I'm buying socks for my dear Mother.
Should I buy these, or find another?"
But Jake's lame ruse was poorly masked.

"Stop frontin', fool!" Lil snapped at Jake.
"You're shopping for no socks for Mom,
but lookin' to bag another fawn.
You're just some gallant on the make!"

Jake saw such fire in Lily's eyes,
he couldn't help but grab her hips,
pulling her close to kiss her lips.
And this temerity proved wise—

his kiss transported Lil to heights
that only Martin could take her to,
so, when he asked her out for brew,
she cocked her head and said "alright."

What's wrong, dear reader, with two suitors?
Best let the better prove himself,
then leave the lesser on the shelf,
to mourn her charm, and miss her hooters.

Jake was spontaneous and fun,
surprising her with morning Danish,
plus poems for her that he'd just finished,
bursting with wit and wicked pun.

And he loved to kiss at traffic stops,
flipping off those who honked their horn,
and, when pulled over, masked his scorn
by charming even the frowning cops.

While Martin took her to hear Mahler,
buying her chocolate and champagne,
sparking libido, heart, and brain,
(though she didn't, quite yet, let him ball her.)

And with his PhD in lit,
plus one more in biology,
Martin was most impressed to see
Lil's native, autodidact wit.

Now, Lil had made no promises,
yet fretted when they might encounter,
and battle o'er who'd get to mount' er,
'bout who would finally make her his.

For instance, strolling Windansea
one day, with Jake, hand in his hand,
Lil spotted Martin, on the sand,
lost in Hegel's philosophy.

"Who's that?" Jake noticed Lily's stare.
"Oh that's just Martin. He's a friend,"
said Lil, and grabbed Jake's jealous hand,
leading him, quickly, out of there.

One other time, while at *Whole Foods*,
'twas Jake who spotted Lil, in line,
flirty, and fresh-faced, looking fine,
and kissing that goddamn Martin dude!

On seeing that, Jake went home fuming,
while Martin had his own suspicions;
it would only take the right conditions
to spark the conflagration looming.

Indeed, one morn, they both showed up
at Lil's, each off'ring coffee and buns.
"But I only need one serving, huns!"
Lil took Jake's bun, and Martin's cup.

But this diplomacy fell flat.
Lil's suitors butted like wild boars.
Jake blustered, "Pal, Lil's mine, not yours!"
While Martin roared, "Lil's mine, take that!"

"Stop now," Lil cried, "or both will lose
whatever hopes you had of me!
I've made no promise yet, you see?
A woman needs some time to choose."

Jake scoffed, "He'll only bore you silly,"
while Martin countered, "Get a shave,
then bathe, then crawl back to your cave!"
Then both shared blows, in front of Lily.

The village was small, their egos great.
Lil knew that one might kill the other,
as jealous Cain knocked off his brother.
She better choose 'fore it's too late!

But how could she make up her mind?
Luckily, Lily's good friend, Lola,
was tarot master of La Jolla,
and she could see, where Lil was blind.

Lo drew the first card in the cross—
"The Two of Cups. This is the present.
It means romance, piteous or pleasant,
leading to happiness or loss."

Lo drew more cards. Some made Lil smile;
some made her fear the fate to come.
Some seemed completely clear, and some
were maddeningly versatile.

Card number seven was the Fool,
suggesting madcap possibilities.
"I see," Lo said, "you're feeling ill at ease.
but sometimes happenstance must rule."

Soon Lola picked choice thrice-times-thrice,
where, fear and hope, the card portends.
"This is the Tower, where something ends,
where winning demands a sacrifice."

"But who will be my own heart's twain,
and who," cried Lil, "will I refuse?
Why must woman be forced to choose,
'tween one man's joy and one man's pain?"

Card number ten was Knight of Swords,
a wily, rash, impassioned rake.
"That must," Lil cried, "be poet Jake,
and Martin's loss is Jake's reward!"

Now don't, dear reader, mourn for Martin;
he found true love with someone else.
In fact, I snagged him for myself!
And this is where we must be partin';

127

who knows if Lil will stay with Jake?
I can't bring you another tip.
Your narrator must now jump ship,
for her self-preservation's sake!